Ready, Set, Snow!

by ABBY KLEIN

illustrated by
JOHN MCKINLEY

THE BLUE SKY PRESS
An Imprint of Scholastic Inc. • New York

To Dani and Josh,
You finally got to experience
your first snow day! Yeah!
Lots of Love,
Mooka

THE BLUE SKY PRESS

Text copyright © 2009 by Abby Klein
Illustrations copyright © 2009 by John McKinley
All rights reserved.

Special thanks to Robert Martin Staenberg.

No part of this publication may be reproduced, stored in
a retrieval system, or transmitted in any form or by any means,
electronic, mechanical, photocopying, recording, or otherwise,
without written permission of the publisher. For information
regarding permission, please write to: Permissions Department,
Scholastic Inc., 557 Broadway, New York, New York 10012.
SCHOLASTIC, THE BLUE SKY PRESS, and associated logos are
trademarks and/or registered trademarks of Scholastic Inc.
Library of Congress catalog card number: 2008034299
ISBN-13: 978-0-439-89596-5 / ISBN-10: 0-439-89596-0
10 9 8 7 6 5 4 3 2 1   09 10 11 12 13 14
Printed in the United States of America 40
First printing, January 2009

CHAPTERS

I have a problem.

A really, really, big problem.

I have to compete in

the Snowshoe Race in the

first-grade Winter Olympics,

but I've never been on

snowshoes in my life!

Let me tell you about it.

CHAPTER 1

Good Sports

"Boys and girls," said our teacher, Mrs. Wushy, "Friday is a very special day."

"Oh, I know it is," interrupted Chloe. "My big ballet recital is on Friday. I can hardly wait! I am the star!"

"Does she really think everything is about her?" I whispered to my best friend, Robbie.

"Yep," Robbie whispered back. "Chloe Winters is the center of the universe. Didn't you know that?"

I giggled.

"No one cares about your stupid recital," barked Max, the biggest bully in the whole first grade.

"Max," said Mrs. Wushy. "What did I tell you about using the word *stupid*?"

Max stared at the ground. "You said I wasn't allowed to say it."

"That is correct. I told you that I don't ever want to hear that word. You need to apologize to Chloe, and you will have a time-out on the bench at recess."

"But . . . that's not fair," groaned Max.

"It's very fair," replied Mrs. Wushy. "Now tell Chloe you're sorry."

Chloe turned to Max. "I'm waiting . . ."

Max just glared at her.

"Mrs. Wushy said you have to say you're sorry, so . . . I'm waiting."

Max mumbled something that no one could hear.

"What did you say?" Chloe asked. "It's not an apology if I can't hear you."

"Max," said Mrs. Wushy, "you're wasting our time. You need to apologize nicely to Chloe right now, or I'm sending you to Mr. Pendergast's office."

I guess Max was not in the mood to have a little chat with the principal, so he quickly spit out, "I'm sorry."

"Thank you, Max. Now I'd like to get back to telling you all about our special day, if everyone is ready to listen."

"We're ready! We're ready!" we all chanted.

"This coming Friday, we are going to have a contest with Room 4."

"A contest? What kind of contest?" asked my friend Jessie. "Do we get to race?"

Jessie was really good at sports. She could probably beat most of the kids in the whole first grade, boys and girls.

"We are going to have a mini Winter Olympics."

"Winter Olympics," said Chloe. "I love the Winter Olympics. The ice-skaters look so beautiful in their fancy costumes. I have a costume just like that I can wear on Friday."

"Ice-skating? Costume? Where does she come up with this stuff?" Robbie whispered. "Does she understand that we are going to do this at school?"

I twirled my finger by my head, making the cuckoo sign.

"I'm sure your costume is beautiful, Chloe, but you won't need it on Friday. Our Olympics are not exactly like the real Olympics."

"Bummer," grumbled Max. "That doesn't sound like very much fun."

"Oh, it will be lots of fun," said Mrs. Wushy. "Our two classes will compete in different events, and whichever class wins the most events will be the winner."

"What are the events going to be, Mrs. Wushy?" asked Jessie.

"Let's see . . . there is the Snowball Toss, where we see who can throw a snowball the farthest."

"I can throw snowballs really far," said Max. "That will be a piece of cake."

"There's the Sled Pull, where you are in teams of two, and one partner sits on the sled while the other person pulls him or her around the track. The first team to cross the finish line wins the race."

"Cool," said Max. "I'm really strong. I know I'll come in first."

"There's the Snowshoe Race, where you have to put on snowshoes and do one lap around the whole school."

"No problem," said Max. "I'm really fast on snowshoes."

"And there's the Snowball Pileup, where we

see how many snowballs you can pile on top of each other before the stack falls over."

"I bet I can pile up more than twenty," said Max.

"You can stop bragging now," said Chloe.

"I am not bragging," replied Max.

"Oh yes you are!"

"Oh no I'm not!"

"Yes you are!"

"No I'm not!"

Mrs. Wushy clapped her hands together. "That is enough, you two. You both need to be quiet. Now, Max," continued Mrs. Wushy, "each student will only be competing in one event. Remember, our class is a team. We need to work together. We are competing against Room 4, not each other. And I expect everyone to show good sportsmanship. Who knows what that means?"

Jessie raised her hand.

"Yes, Jessie."

"Showing good sportsmanship means that
you are a good sport. You play by the rules,
and you play fair."

Robbie raised his hand.

"Yes, Robbie."

"You try to win, but if you lose, you don't

whine or complain. You always congratulate
the other team."

"Excellent, Robbie," said Mrs. Wushy.
"Anyone else?"

Chloe's hand shot up.

"Here we go again," Jessie whispered.

"Being a good sport means you don't brag

to the other team, and you don't call people names," Chloe said, glaring at Max.

"You are all right," said Mrs. Wushy. "And on Friday you will all get a chance to show me what good sports you are, win or lose."

"We're gonna win!" we all chanted. "We're gonna win!"

"I'm glad you are all so excited about it."

"I want to do the Snowshoe Race," Max blurted out.

"I'm sorry, Max, but we've run out of time. We have to get to lunch. I will have the sign-ups ready after lunch, so you all have a little bit of time to think about what event you want to compete in."

I let out a sigh of relief. At least I wouldn't be in a race with Max. There was no way I was signing up for the Snowshoe Race. I had never been on snowshoes in my life. For once, things seemed to be going my way.

CHAPTER 2

The Bet

As soon as we sat down to lunch, everyone started talking about the Winter Olympics.

"I can't wait until Friday," said Jessie. "I don't know what I'm going to sign up for. All the events sound like so much fun!"

"Well, you can sign up for anything," I said to Jessie, "because you are so good at sports."

"You are, too, Freddy."

Max snorted. "Are you kidding me? Him?

Good at sports?" he said, laughing and pointing his finger at me.

"Why are you laughing, Max?" said Jessie. "For your information, Freddy is the best dodgeball player in first grade."

"No he's not. I am."

"Yeah, right," I muttered under my breath.

Max whipped his head around. "What did you say, wimp?"

I froze. He wasn't supposed to hear me. Did he have some kind of supersonic hearing? "Uh . . . uh . . . uh . . ." I stammered.

Max grabbed me by the shirt. "I said, 'What did you say?'"

"Nothing," I squeaked.

"You said something, and I want to know what it was right now, or else!" he said, tightening his grip on my shirt.

"Or else what?" Jessie butted in. "Let go of him, Max, you big bully."

"And what if I don't?"

Jessie got right in Max's face. "Let go of him . . . right . . . now, or you'll have to deal with me. Got it?"

Max looked at Jessie. Then he looked at me, and then he looked back at Jessie. Something in her eyes must have told him it would not be a good idea to mess with her, so he slowly let go of my shirt.

I scooted over closer to Robbie.

"Boy, Jessie is so brave," whispered Robbie.

"I know. I wish I could stand up to Max like she does."

"So, Freddy," Jessie continued as if nothing had happened, "what do you think you are going to sign up for?"

I took a bite of my peanut-butter sandwich. "I'm not sure yet," I said, licking the peanut butter off my fingers. "How about you?"

"I think I'm going to sign up for the Sled Pull," Chloe interrupted. "Do you want to be my partner, Jessie?"

"You're going to pull Jessie?" Max said, laughing. "I can't wait to see that!"

"I'm not going to pull her, silly. I was just going to sit on the sled and let her pull me."

"Figures," Robbie mumbled.

"My nana got me a handmade scarf and mittens from Sweden. I could sit on the sled and look cute."

"Is she for real?" said Robbie.

Jessie stared at Chloe for a minute and then said, "Sorry, but I was planning on signing up for the Snowball Toss."

"That's for boys."

"Says who?"

"Throwing snowballs is like throwing a baseball, and everyone knows that only boys play baseball," said Chloe.

"Well, little Miss Know-It-All, I play on a baseball team, and I am the pitcher. I can throw the ball better than any of the boys on my team."

Chloe stared at Jessie for a minute. "Oh," she said. "Well, then. I guess I'll just have to find another partner."

"Good luck with that," Robbie muttered under his breath.

"So, Freddy, you still haven't told us what you're going to sign up for," said Max. "I bet you're going to do the Snowball Stack. That's an easy thing for a wimp like you."

"You first, Max," Jessie said. "Why don't you tell us what you're going to do?"

"I'm going to do the hardest thing in the whole Olympics."

"Oh yeah? What's that?"

"The Snowshoe Race. I bet no one else in the class can do that, so I'll have to win that event for our class."

"Why do you think you're the only one who can do that?" asked Jessie. "Freddy is really fast on snowshoes."

I kicked Jessie under the table and whispered, "No I'm not."

"What did he say?"

"He said he thinks he can beat you," said Jessie.

"Oh really?" Max said, smiling. "Hey, Shark Boy, wanna bet?"

I gulped. I did not know how to use snowshoes, but I didn't want to seem like a wimp in front of Max. If I didn't take the bet, he would keep teasing me. "Uh . . . sure . . . What do you want to bet?"

Robbie tapped me on the leg. "Are you crazy? You don't even own a pair of snowshoes. What are you doing?"

I ignored Robbie.

"I bet you your dessert for a whole week," said Max.

My dessert for a whole week! Dessert was my favorite part of my lunch, and I really didn't want to watch Max eating it.

"Earth to Freddy. Earth to Freddy," Robbie said, waving his hand in front of my face. "What are you doing? You cannot beat Max Sellars."

"So, Freddy, is it a bet or not? I don't have all day," said Max.

"It's a bet!" I said quickly before I could change my mind.

"Oh no!" Robbie groaned softly. "What did you just do?"

"I'm not sure," I whispered. "I'm not sure."

Jessie pumped her fist in the air. "Way to go, Freddy!"

I smiled. Then I turned to her and whispered, "There's only one problem."

"What's that?"

"I've never been on snowshoes in my whole life!"

CHAPTER 3

You What?

That night at dinner my mom asked, "So, anything interesting happen at school today?"

"Freddy made a bet," my sister, Suzie, blurted out.

I stared at her. "What?" I asked, trying to sound as if I had no idea what she was even talking about.

"Freddy made a bet with Max Sellars."

"Why did you make a bet with Max Sellars?" asked my mom.

"Who said I made a bet with Max?"

"Julie, that brown-haired girl in your class, told me today after school."

Boy, news travels fast! Why did Julie have to go blab to my sister?

"So, Freddy, is this true?" said my dad. "Did you make a bet with Max?"

"I . . . uh . . . I . . . uh . . ."

"It's a simple question. Yes or no. Did you make a bet?"

"Yes," I mumbled.

"What's the bet?"

"I bet that I could beat him in the Snowshoe Race in the first-grade Winter Olympics."

"Ha, ha, ha." Suzie laughed hysterically. "That's the funniest thing I've ever heard in my life!"

"What's so funny about it?"

"You've never even been on snowshoes."

"So?"

"So you expect to race the biggest, toughest kid in first grade and win when you don't even know how to put the snowshoes on? Ha, ha, ha." She was laughing so hard I thought she was going to fall out of her chair.

"Stop laughing!"

"But . . . but . . . it's so funny."

"Be quiet, brat!"

"Ha, ha, ha."

"Stop it!"

"All right. Enough, you two," said my dad. "Suzie, you need to stop laughing at your brother, and, Freddy, you need to start from the beginning, and tell us what this is all about."

"Well," I began, "the first-grade Winter Olympics is on Friday."

"What's that?" asked my mom.

"Don't you remember, Mom?" I said. "Suzie did it when she was in Mrs. Wushy's class."

"Yeah," said Suzie. "Room 3 and Room 4 compete against each other in some silly snow games, and whichever class wins the most events wins the trophy."

"Oh yes, I remember now," said my dad. "When you were in Mrs. Wushy's class, you did the snowball stacking game."

"Yep."

"How many snowballs did you stack before they fell over?"

"I stacked eleven snowballs."

"Wow!" I said. "That's a lot!"

"I thought for sure I was going to win, but then Dani Klein from Room 4 stacked twelve and won."

"So, Freddy," said my mom, "why didn't you sign up for snowball stacking? I'm sure Suzie would have helped you practice that."

"I was going to, but then Max started teasing me at lunch."

"It seems like that's all that boy ever does," said my mom.

"You can say that again," I said. "Anyway, he kept laughing at me and calling me a wimp."

"Why don't you just ignore him, honey?"

"I was trying to, but Jessie was really mad that he kept teasing me. When he bragged that he was better at snowshoeing than I was, Jessie told him that I could beat him any day. I tried to tell her that I have never even been on snowshoes, but she just kept right on talking."

"So now what are you going to do?"

"I don't have a choice. I have to learn how to snowshoe in three days, or I'll never be able to show my face again at school."

"How are you going to do that, genius?" said Suzie. "You don't even own a pair of snowshoes."

"Robbie said I could borrow his, and he and Jessie are going to come over after school tomorrow and teach me."

"That's very nice of them to do that."

"Ugh," I groaned, putting my face in my hands. "I'm never going to be able to learn in three days." Just then my elbow slipped, and my face fell in my plate.

Again, Suzie started laughing hysterically. "Ha, ha, ha, ha, ha!"

My mom rushed over and pulled my head out of my plate. "Oh my goodness, Freddy! Look at you!"

My face was covered in mashed potatoes

and gravy, and there were little pieces of corn
stuck in my hair.

"Stay right there. Don't move. I'm going to
get something to wash you off."

I scraped some of the mashed potatoes off
my cheek and licked my finger. "Mmm, it still
tastes pretty good."

"Ewww. That's gross," Suzie whined.

"What's gross?" said my mom as she returned to the table carrying a sponge and paper towels.

"Freddy just ate some mashed potatoes off his face!"

"Freddy, where are your manners? That is disgusting! You do not eat food off your face! Now look at me so I can wipe you off."

My mom wiped the gravy and potatoes off my face and pulled the corn kernels out of my hair. "That's good for now, but you'll have to take an extra long bath tonight."

"Awwww, Mom," I groaned. "You know I hate taking baths."

"Too bad, mister. That's what happens when you decide to wear your food. Please try to be more careful next time."

"Yes, Mom."

"So, Freddy," said my dad, "don't be so upset."

"Don't be so upset! Don't be so upset!" I shouted. "The biggest bully in the whole first grade is going to kick my butt in front of the class, and you're telling me not to be upset!"

"Calm down. There's no need to yell. Your friends said they would teach you how to snowshoe."

"But I only have three days! There's no way I can learn in three days!"

"Remember when you had to learn to ride a two-wheeler in a week, and you never thought you'd be able to do that?"

"Yeah."

"Well you did, didn't you? And not only did you learn to ride, you rode more laps than Max did that day."

"I guess so."

"You can learn anything as long as you set your mind to it."

"I don't know, Dad," I said, shaking my head. "I just don't know."

CHAPTER 4

Training

The next day after school, Robbie and Jessie came over to teach me how to snowshoe. Before we headed outside, we stopped in the kitchen for a snack.

"Hi, Mom. It sure smells good in here."

"Hi, Mrs. Thresher. Whatever you made smells amazing," said Robbie.

Jessie's eyes got big and wide. "Are those homemade brownies?"

"Yes, they are," said my mom. "I thought

you might need some extra energy for your training session today, so I made you a special treat."

"These brownies are delicious, Mrs. Thresher," Robbie said, taking a big bite.

"Thank you, Robbie."

"Yeah, they're yummy," agreed Jessie, licking her lips.

"Well, I think it's very sweet of both of you to help Freddy learn how to snowshoe. Freddy, you are lucky to have such nice friends."

"It's no problem," said Robbie. "I brought my snowshoes for Freddy to borrow, and Jessie is going to help him with his speed."

"Jessie is probably the fastest kid in the whole school," I said.

"I don't think the whole school," Jessie said, laughing.

"Well, you're faster than anybody in the whole first grade."

We each shoved another brownie in our mouths and gulped down a glass of milk.

"Okay, Freddy, ready to go?" asked Jessie.

"I guess I'm as ready as I'll ever be."

"It's cold out there today, kids," said my mom, "so bundle up. Freddy, do you want to wear your snow pants?"

"Snow pants? I don't really plan on getting my pants wet."

"But what if you fall down?"

"Fall down? I don't plan on falling down, Mom. I'm not going skiing."

"It's up to you. Just make sure you keep your mittens on. I don't want your fingers to get too cold."

"Sure thing, Mom. Come on, guys. Let's get started."

We put on our snowboots, Robbie grabbed the snowshoes, and we headed outside.

"Brrrr, it's cold out today," I said, shivering.

I breathed out a puff of air. "Hey, look, you can see my breath."

"It looks like dragon smoke," said Robbie.

"Do you think there really are dragons?" asked Jessie.

"There is no scientific evidence," Robbie explained. Robbie knows everything about everything. He is like a science genius. "They're just made-up creatures from stories."

"That's too bad because I'd love to see a real one," Jessie said.

"Enough about dragons," said Robbie. "Let's get started. First, you have to stick your foot in here," he said, pointing to a little opening at the front of the snowshoe. "Just like you're putting on a slipper. Then you tighten this strap around your ankle. It's really very easy."

Robbie put the two snowshoes on the ground, and I slipped my feet into the holes. "So far, so good."

"Now just fix the strap around your ankle. You want to make sure it's tight enough so that it doesn't fall off."

When I bent to tighten the strap, I fell over and landed in the snow.

"Ha, ha, ha," Jessie giggled. "You don't

snowshoe on your butt, Freddy. You have to stay on your feet."

"Very funny," I said as I got back up.

"Sometimes I bend down and put one knee in the snow to help me balance while I tighten the strap on the other foot," said Robbie.

"Good idea," I said. I got down on one knee and fixed the strap. Then I switched sides and did the other strap.

"Ready, Freddy?" asked Jessie.

"As ready as I'll ever be."

"Okay," said Robbie. "Now just start walking like you normally do, but make sure you keep a little space between your feet, so the snowshoes don't get caught on each other."

"Okeydokey." I took two steps and fell flat on my face. Jessie laughed.

I sat up and wiped the snow out of my eyes and mouth.

"You're supposed to walk in the snow, not eat it."

"Very funny."

"Here, let me help you up," said Robbie. He gave me his hand and pulled me up. "Remember what I said. Just make sure you keep a little bit of space between your snowshoes."

This time I went about four steps before my feet crossed over each other, and I crashed. "I'm never going to be able to do the race," I moaned.

"Yes you are," said Jessie. "Just get up and try again."

This time I think I took about ten steps before crashing.

"See?" said Robbie. "You're already doing a lot better."

"But I still keep landing on my butt."

"Don't give up. It just takes practice."

After about twenty minutes, I was able to go pretty far without falling down.

"Now it's time to try running," said Jessie.

"Running? Are you crazy? I can't run in these things."

"Yes you can, Freddy. You just lift your feet up a little more than you usually do when you run. Like this. Watch me." Jessie ran once around the yard. "Now you try it."

To my surprise, running was actually a little easier than walking.

"You're doing great!" said Robbie. "Don't stop! Keep going."

I almost made it once around the yard before I fell on my back.

Jessie and Robbie came running over. "Are you all right?" they asked together.

"Yeah. I think so, but could you guys help me up? I think I'm stuck."

They each took one of my hands and helped me up.

"That was awesome!" said Jessie. "You're really getting the hang of it. I think we should start timing you now and working on your speed."

"Whatever you say, coach," I said, smiling.

Robbie pulled a little notebook and stopwatch out of his pocket. "Jessie, you help Freddy with his form, and I'll keep track of his times in my notebook."

We must have stayed outside training for about two hours.

When it started to get dark, I said, "Uh, guys."

"Yeah?"

"My feet are so cold, I don't think I can feel my toes anymore."

"Well, I think that's enough training for today. Let's go in."

"So, how did it go?" asked my mom.

"It went great, Mrs. Thresher," said Jessie. "If we practice every afternoon this week, Freddy is going to win that race."

CHAPTER 5

The Big Day

On Friday morning I couldn't sleep. I was
excited and nervous about the race. I jumped
out of bed and started to get dressed. Mrs.
Wushy had told us all to wear red shirts and
red hats. We were going to be the red team,
and Mrs. Brown's class was going to be the
blue team.

I opened three different drawers, but I
couldn't find my red shirt anywhere. I sat
down on the edge of my bed and hit my

forehead with the palm of my hand. "Think, think, think!" Oh no! I just remembered that I wore it two days ago and forgot to ask my mom to wash it. I ran to the bathroom to look in the dirty clothes hamper, but the door was locked as usual.

"Hey, open up!" I yelled, pounding on the door.

No answer.

I pounded on the door again. "Hey, Princess Poopyhead, stop looking at yourself in the mirror, and open the door!"

"Go away, Shark Boy. I'm in here now," she yelled back.

I banged on the door again, and this time Suzie made the mistake of opening the door a crack to yell at me. I was able to squeeze my way in.

"Hey, get out of here, creep!"

"Not until I find my red shirt," I said, throwing clothes out of the hamper.

"Hey, watch it. You just threw a pair of your dirty underwear in my face!"

"Ah, here it is," I said, holding up my red shirt.

"You can't wear that."

"Why not?"

"Because it's dirty."

"So?"

"Mom, the Queen of Clean, would not be too happy if she found out you were wearing a dirty shirt."

"But today is the Winter Olympics, and Mrs. Wushy said that we have to wear red shirts. Besides, Mom will never know."

"Unless someone tells her."

"You wouldn't do that," I said, looking Suzie straight in the eye.

"What's it worth to you?"

"Are you kidding me?"

Suzie just stared at me with her hands on her hips.

"OK, OK, just tell me what you want."

"You make my bed for three days, and I won't tell Mom you're wearing a dirty shirt." She held up her pinkie for a pinkie swear.

"Three days?"

"I could make it four."

"Fine," I said. "It's a deal. I'll make your bed for three days."

We locked pinkies. "Deal," said Suzie. "Now get out of the bathroom. Your breath stinks. It smells like shark breath."

"How would you know what that smells like?" I shouted as I ran back to my room.

"Freddy, is that you?" my mom called from downstairs. "You need to get a move on. You don't want to be late to school."

"Coming, Mom," I yelled. I threw on my pants, grabbed my red hat, and ran downstairs.

"Good morning, honey. I made you a special breakfast today—French toast and bacon."

"Thanks, Mom. It looks yummy," I said, stuffing a forkful into my mouth.

Just then Suzie came into the kitchen. "Smells good, Mom."

My mom gave Suzie her breakfast, and then she turned to me. "Freddy, didn't you just wear that shirt two days ago? I haven't washed since then."

I gulped. I looked at Suzie, and she looked at me. I mouthed the words, "We have a deal."

"Uh, actually, Mom," said Suzie, "that was Robbie. He was wearing his red Lincoln Elementary shirt when he was over here the other day helping Freddy train for the race."

"Oh, I could have sworn it was Freddy, but I guess you're right."

"Thanks," I mouthed to Suzie.

She just smiled back.

I looked at the clock. "Oh no! The bus is going to be here any minute. I don't want to be late."

I jumped out of my chair, tripped over my backpack, and went sailing to the floor.

My mom came running over. "Freddy, are you all right?"

I sat up slowly and did a quick check of my knees and elbows. "Yeah, I'm fine. I just hope I don't do that in the middle of the race. That would be so embarrassing!"

"And hilarious!" Suzie added.

"Suzie," said my dad, "that wasn't a nice thing to say. Apologize to your brother."

"But . . ."

"Suzie . . ."

"Sorry, Freddy."

"Now wish him luck."

"Good luck, Freddy. I hope you beat Max. And I mean that."

"Thanks. I'll try."

"Don't worry, honey. You'll be great!" said my mom.

I grabbed my backpack and the snowshoes and ran toward the door. "Go get 'em, Mouse. You're a winner!" my dad called after me.

"You're a winner. You're a winner," I muttered to myself as I slammed the front door and jumped on the bus.

As I plopped down in my seat, I heard a voice say, "Hello, loser. Ready for the race?"

CHAPTER 6

Team Captain

It seemed as if the bus ride took forever. Max just kept bragging about how he was going to beat me. I thought we were never going to get to school.

When the bus pulled into the parking lot, I jumped off and ran to the classroom. Outside the door was a huge sign that said WELCOME TO THE WINTER OLYMPICS.

"Cool," I said.

"Very cool," said Jessie. "I can't wait!"

We all went inside and quickly sat down on the rug.

"Good morning, boys and girls," said Mrs. Wushy. "Today is the big day. I hope you all are ready."

"Oh, I'm ready," said Chloe. "I've got my new hat, scarf, and mittens. See how they all match?"

"But your hat is pink," said Max. "Everyone's supposed to wear red, not pink."

"But then I wouldn't match," said Chloe. "And for your information, this color pink is called baby pink, and a red hat would not look good with the baby pink scarf and these mittens."

"Does she know this is an athletic event, not a fashion show?" Jessie whispered.

"It's always about the outfits," Robbie answered.

"I did ask everyone to wear red," said Mrs. Wushy. "I wanted us to look like a team."

"Well, my fingernails are painted red," Chloe said, waving her fingers in the air.

"Whoop-de-doo," said Max. "That will help us win today for sure."

Mrs. Wushy stared at Chloe for a minute, and then she continued. "Before we start the

Olympics today, each team must choose a team captain."

"I think I should be the team captain," said Max.

"Is he kidding?" whispered Robbie.

"Me, me, me!" Max shouted, jumping up and down.

"Well," said Mrs. Wushy, "this is how it's

going to work. First, children in the class will suggest some people that they think would make a good team captain, and then the class will vote."

"Vote for me! Vote for me!" yelled Max.

"Max, you need to stop shouting out. If you can't control yourself, then I will have to ask you to leave the room."

"OK," Max said quietly.

"Now remember, the team captain must always play by the rules, be a good sport, and support his or her teammates."

Jessie raised her hand.

"Yes, Jessie."

"I think Robbie should be the team captain because he always plays by the rules, and he is very smart."

"Excellent, Jessie. I agree. Anyone else?"

I raised my hand.

"Freddy, do you have a suggestion?"

"Yes, Mrs. Wushy. I think Jessie should be the team captain because she is really good at sports, she never cheats, and she is always nice to everyone in the class."

After some other kids in the class made a few more suggestions, and Mrs. Wushy added their names to the list, it was time to vote.

"Okay," said Mrs. Wushy. "I think it's time to vote."

"But what about me?" Chloe whined.

"What about you?"

"No one suggested me for team captain."

"That's because you're lame," said Max.

"Oh! Did you hear that, Mrs. Wushy? Did you hear what he just said to me?"

"Yes, I did. Max, that was very rude. Because of that, I am taking your name off the list for team captain. A team captain would not treat other people like that, and if you don't stop calling people names, then you won't be allowed to participate in the Olympics. Instead, you can spend that time in Mr. Pendergast's office. Do you understand?"

Max just looked at her, but he didn't say anything.

"Max, I am asking you a question, and I expect an answer. I will ask you one more time. Do you understand?"

"Yes," he muttered.

"Good. Now I think we're ready to vote. Remember, boys and girls, you may only vote once, and you are voting for someone who you think shows good sportsmanship and is a good leader."

"But what if I like more than one person?" asked Chloe.

"You have to choose one," said Mrs. Wushy. "I will say the names one at a time. You raise your hand for the person you want to be the team captain. Any questions?"

No one raised a hand.

"Good. I want this to be a secret vote, so close your eyes. No peeking. Here we go."

Mrs. Wushy said the names one at a time. It was really hard for me to decide who to vote for because Robbie and Jessie are both good friends of mine.

After Mrs. Wushy finished reading all the names, she told us to open our eyes. "I think you all made a good choice. This person will make a great team captain."

"I wish she would just say the name already," whispered Jessie.

"I know what you mean," said Robbie. "My stomach is doing flip-flops."

"Good luck, you guys," I whispered.

"Thanks, Freddy."

"The team captain for Room 3 will be . . . Jessie Sanchez."

The class clapped.

"As the team captain, you get to wear this

special pin on your hat. Come on up, so I can put it on."

Jessie got up and proudly walked to the front of the room.

"Now that we have our team captain," Mrs. Wushy said, "it looks like we're ready to go. Everyone, grab your coat and line up behind your captain. Let's go show Room 4 what we're made of!"

CHAPTER 7

Go, Team!

When we got outside, Room 4 was already there waiting for us. I gulped. Some of the kids in that class looked really big.

"Before we get started, boys and girls," said Mrs. Wushy and Mrs. Brown, "you all must take the athlete's oath. Raise your right hand and repeat after us."

We all raised our right hands.

"I promise to play by the rules and be a good sport."

"I promise to play by the rules and be a good sport," we all repeated.

"Let the games begin!"

"Is the Snowshoe Race first?" asked Max.

"No. The first event is the Snowball Stack. Everyone who is participating in that event, please step forward."

Robbie had signed up, and he was really good at making the perfect snowball. He knew exactly how to pack the snow so it wouldn't fall apart.

"OK, the person who can stack the most snowballs wins. On your mark, get set, go!"

All the kids started making snowballs as fast as they could and stacking them up. Most of the kids only got about seven or eight in their stack before it fell over. Only Robbie and a girl named Jen from Mrs. Brown's class were left. Robbie was already up to ten snowballs, and he was still going.

"Come on, Robbie. You can do it!" I yelled.

"Robb-ie, Robb-ie, Robb-ie!" the class chanted.

When Jen put on her next snowball, her stack started to wiggle, but it didn't fall over.

"That makes eleven for Jen," said Mrs. Brown smiling.

Robbie carefully put on snowball number eleven. His stack didn't even move.

"We're going to win this for sure," I said to Jessie. "Robbie is so good at this."

As soon as Jen went to place her twelfth snowball on top, her whole stack toppled over.

"Awwwww!" moaned Room 4.

"Robbie still has to put on number twelve for us to win this event," said Mrs. Wushy.

I held my breath.

Robbie slowly placed snowball number twelve on the stack and stepped back. The pile wobbled slightly, but it did not fall over.

"That's a winner," said Mrs. Wushy.

We all cheered.

"Way to go, Robbie," I said, patting him on the back.

"That's one point for Room 3. Time for the next event, the Long Jump."

In this event, the teachers were just going to measure who could jump the farthest in snow boots. The students jumped one at a time. Room 4 has a boy named Josh who has the longest legs you've ever seen. He easily jumped farther than anyone. No one else even came close.

"The score is one point for Room 3, and one point for Room 4."

"That wasn't really fair," Max grumbled. "His legs were so long."

"That's OK," said Jessie. "Come on, Room 3. Let's win the next event."

"That's the way to encourage your team," said Mrs. Wushy.

"The next event is the Snowball Toss," said

Mrs. Brown. "If you are in this event, please stand on this line."

Jessie walked to the line.

"Come on, everybody," I said. "Let's cheer for our team captain."

"Jess-ie, Jess-ie, Jess-ie!"

The kids took turns throwing. A boy named Nick in Mrs. Brown's class threw the ball so far, it landed next to the fence on the edge of the playground.

"Wow!" I whispered to Robbie. "That went really far."

"I know. We might be in trouble."

"I bet you can't beat that, little girl," Nick said to Jessie.

"Oh yes she can!" I yelled back.

"Yes she can! Yes she can!" the whole class started to chant.

Jessie took a step back, lifted her arm, and threw with all her might. The snowball sailed over the playground fence into the street.

"I'd say that's a winner," said Mrs. Brown. We all screamed and cheered.

"That makes the score two to one in favor of Mrs. Wushy's class. Next up is the Sled Pull."

"Oh, that's me! That's me!" shouted Chloe. "Come on, Julie," she said to the only person in the class who would be her partner. "Let's go!"

Chloe sat down in the sled, fixed her hat
and scarf, and smiled a big movie-star smile.
"Now remember, Julie, you have to pull as
hard as you can. We have to come in first."

"On your mark, get set, go!"

Chloe and Julie only got about five feet
when Chloe fell off of the sled. "Oh no! Oh

no! Now look what you've done, Julie. You've ruined the hat and scarf my nana brought me from Sweden!"

"Get back on! Get back on!" we all yelled, but Chloe ignored us and continued to pout, and a team from Mrs. Brown's class crossed the finish line.

"Thanks a lot, Little Miss Priss!" Max yelled. "We lost that event because of you!"

"That's OK, Max," said Jessie. "We'll win the next one."

Jessie was such a good team captain. I'm glad the class chose her.

"The score is tied," said Mrs. Brown. "This last event will decide who wins this year's Winter Olympics."

"Oh great!" I muttered to myself. "Just great!"

I felt a slap on the back and Max's hot breath in my ear. "Time to race, wimp. Let's go!"

CHAPTER 8

The Race

I strapped on my snowshoes and walked to the starting line. I was so nervous I thought I was going to throw up.

"Everybody ready? On your mark, get set, go!" called Mrs. Wushy.

Max took off like a rocket. Boy, was he fast.

I tried to focus on my feet, so my snowshoes wouldn't get caught on each other.

I could hear Jessie and Robbie yelling, "Come on, Freddy! You can do it!"

My heart was pounding so hard I thought it was going to pop out of my chest.

I wasn't sure I could make it all the way around the school.

The classes were chanting, "Room 3! Room 4! Room 3! Room 4!"

I looked up to see how much farther I had to go, and that's when I saw it . . . Max fell flat on his face. I couldn't believe it! It was my lucky day!

As I got closer to him, I could see that he was struggling to get up, but his strap was caught in the other snowshoe.

I could have run right by him and won

the bet, but then I thought about what Mrs. Wushy had said about being a good sport. I wouldn't be a very good teammate if I just left him there and didn't help.

I stopped running and bent down to help Max untangle his strap.

"What are you doing?" asked Max.

"Helping you. Your strap is caught in your other snowshoe."

Max just stared at me for a minute. I think for the first time in his life he didn't have anything to say.

I untangled the strap. "There you go," I said. "It's all fixed. You can get up now." I reached out to help him up.

"But . . . but . . . but . . . what about the bet?" he asked. "And why are you being so nice to me?"

"Because we're teammates, and that's what teammates do. They help each other."

When we were both on our feet again, Max whispered, "You go ahead, Freddy. You should be the winner."

I took off like lightning. A boy in Mrs. Brown's class had passed me when I stopped to help Max. I had to catch up to him if I had any chance of winning the race.

I took a deep breath and ran with all my

might. "You can do it! You can do it!" I said to myself.

I could hear my classmates cheering for me: "Fredd-y, Fredd-y, Fredd-y!"

The other boy and I were neck and neck. I gave one last push and beat him over the finish line by a hair. Then I collapsed on the ground.

All the kids in the class came rushing over and piled on top of me.

"Freddy, you're our hero!"

I smiled.

"Come on over here, boys and girls. It's time to award the trophy," said our teachers.

We all gathered around.

"This year the Winter Olympics trophy goes to Mrs. Wushy's class. Congratulations to everyone for your hard work."

We all cheered. "We're number one! We're number one!"

"I am so proud of you," said Mrs. Wushy, "and I am especially proud of Freddy. He really showed us today what it means to be a team-mate and taught us what good sportsmanship is all about. And that is more important than any trophy."

I smiled a big smile and winked at Max. And for once, I think he may have smiled back.

When I was little, my elementary school held an Olympics competition every year. I grew up in California, so we couldn't do any winter sports like Freddy and his friends did. We had running races, a hitting and pitching contest, and even special events like a hopscotch tournament.

I loved playing hopscotch. I used to play it with my friends every day at recess. When I was in fourth grade, I decided to enter the hopscotch tournament in the Olympics, and to my surprise, I came in first place!

I hope you have as much fun reading *Ready, Set, Snow!* as I had writing it.

HAPPY READING!

Freddy's Fun Pages

FREDDY'S SHARK JOURNAL

RECORD BREAKERS

The fastest shark is the mako, which can reach speeds of up to 60 mph.

The shark that lives the longest is the spiny dogfish. It can live to be about 70 years old.

The shark that lives in the coldest waters is the sleeper shark.

The shark that gives birth to the most pups is the whale shark. It can give birth to several hundred pups in one litter.

The rarest shark is the megamouth. Only 14 have ever been seen.

WINTER OLYMPICS TRIVIA

How much do you know about the Winter Olympics? Take this little quiz to find out!

1. When did the first Winter Olympics take place?

2. Which country has won the most gold medals in the Winter Olympics?

3. How many times has Lake Placid hosted the Winter Olympics?

4. Can you name three sports in the Winter Olympics?

5. What was the first tropical island nation to compete in the bobsled event in the Winter Olympics?

6. What is the Olympic motto?

7. Who is the youngest figure skater to win a gold medal?

ANSWERS

1. 1924 2. Norway 3. Two 4. Skiing, snowboarding, luge, bobsled, speed skating, figure skating, hockey 5. Jamaica 6. "Swifter, Higher, Stronger" 7. Tara Lipinski

MARSHMALLOW SNOWMAN

Even if you live where it never snows, here's a snowman that you can make!

YOU WILL NEED:
three large marshmallows
a tube of icing
assorted small candies

one toothpick
one thin pretzel stick
one chocolate kiss

1. Spread icing between the marshmallows and stick them together with the toothpick.

2. Add dots of icing to glue on the candy, and then decorate the face and the body.

3. Break the pretzel stick in half and stick into the sides of the middle marshmallow for arms.

4. Stick the candy kiss on the top marshmallow for a hat.

5. Try drawing on your snow-man with the icing, and enjoy!

SNOWFLAKES

Make these beautiful snowflakes
to decorate your room for winter.

YOU WILL NEED:

popsicle sticks
various shapes of
  dried pasta
white glue

white paint
small paintbrush
glitter
string or yarn

1. Glue two
popsicle sticks
together to
form an "X,"
then glue
one or more
across at a
diagonal.

2. Glue various shapes of dried
pasta on top of the popsicle
sticks. You could use wagon
wheels, bowties, penne, etc.

3. When the glue has dried, paint
the pasta and sticks white.

4. While the paint is still
wet, sprinkle your snowflake
with glitter.

5. Tie or glue a piece of string or yarn around the
top of the snowflake and hang
it up in your room.

Have you read all about Freddy?

Don't miss any of Freddy's
funny adventures!

Ready, Set, Snow!